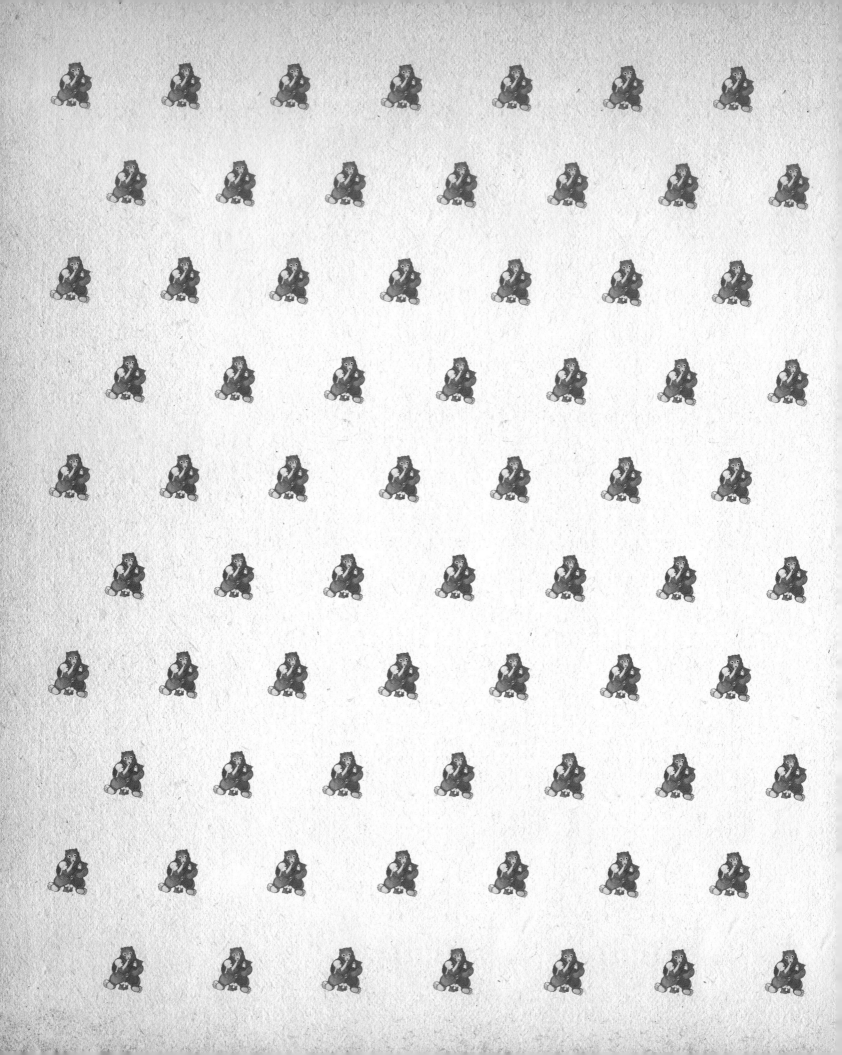

Snow White & Rose Red

Illustrations by Denise Marshall
Book design by Howard Kirk Besserman

© Copyright 2008 Lemniscate, Inc.
All rights reserved.

Published by Bell Pond Books
610 Main Street, Great Barrington, MA 01230
www.bellpondbooks.com

ISBN 978-0-88010-591-0
Library of Congress Cataloging-in-Publication Data is available.
Printed in the United States of America

 Enchantmints Design Studio
w w w . e n c h a n t m i n t s . c o m

Snow White & Rose Red

by The Brothers Grimm

Illustrations by Denise Marshall

Book Design by Howard Kirk Besserman

HA CASS COUNTY PUBLIC LIBRARY
400 E. MECHANIC
HARRISONVILLE, MO 64701

0 0022 0428242 6

nce there was a poor widow who lived in a small cottage by the edge of a forest. In front of the cottage there was a garden where two rose trees grew, one with white roses and the other with red. The widow had two children who were like the two rose trees, one was called Snow White, and the other Rose Red. No two children had ever been as kind and devoted, and as helpful and cheerful, as they were. Rose Red liked to run about in the meadows and fields looking for flowers and catching butterflies. Snow White was more quiet and gentle than Rose Red. She liked to stay at home, helping with the housework and being read to by her mother when all the work was done.

The two children were so fond of one another that they always held each other by the hand when they went out together. When Snow White would say: "We will never leave each other," Rose Red would answer: "Not as long as we live," and their mother would add: "What one has she must share with the other."

They would often go into the woods alone to pick red berries, but they never were afraid of the animals because they made friends with them. The little rabbits would eat cabbage leaves out of their hands, the does grazed beside them, the stags bound right by them, and the birds sat on low branches and sang all the songs they knew.

No harm ever came to them. If they had stayed too late in the forest and night came, they would lie down on the soft moss next to each other and sleep until dawn. Their mother knew this and never worried about them.

Once, after they spent the night in the forest and the rising sun roused them, they saw a beautiful child in a shining white dress sitting near them. The child stood up and looked quite kindly at them, but said nothing and went off into the forest. When they looked around they saw that they had been sleeping close to a cliff, and would certainly have fallen off the edge if they had gone only a few steps farther in the darkness. When their mother heard this she told them that the shining child must have been the angel who watches over good children.

Snow White and Rose Red kept the little cottage so neat and clean that it was a pleasure to look at. In the summer Rose Red took care of the house, and every morning she would put a wreath of flowers with a rose from each tree by her mother's bed. In the winter Snow White lit the fire and hung the kettle over the hearth. The kettle was made of brass, and Snow White had polished it so much that it shone like gold. In the evening, when the snowflakes were falling, the mother would say: "Snow White, go and bolt the door." Then they gathered round the hearth and the mother would put on her spectacles and read to them out of a large book. The two girls listened as they sat and knitted. Close by them, a little lamb lay on the floor, and behind them a little white dove perched with its head tucked under its wings.

ne evening, as they were sitting comfortably together, someone knocked at the door as if he wanted to be let in. The mother said: "Quickly, Rose Red, open the door, it must be a traveler seeking shelter." Rose Red went at once to the door and pushed back the bolt. She was sure that it was going to be some poor soul, but it wasn't at all. It was a big shaggy bear, and he stretched his broad, brown head right through the doorway.

Rose Red screamed and jumped back, the lamb bleated, the dove fluttered into the air, and Snow White hid behind the mother's bed. But the bear began to speak and said: "Don't be afraid, I will not harm you! I am half-frozen from the cold, and only want to warm myself a little beside your fire."

"Poor bear," said the mother. "Lie down by the hearth, only take care that you don't burn your coat." Then she called out: "Snow White, Rose Red, come back, the bear won't hurt you, he means well." So they both came back, and little by little the lamb and the dove came nearer and were not afraid of him. The bear said: "Here, children, knock the snow out of my fur coat." They brought the broom and swept the bear's coat clean. Then he stretched out by the fire and began to rumble contentedly.

It was not long before the children grew quite at ease with the bear, and even began to play tricks on their clumsy guest. They tugged at his fur and put their feet on his back. They rolled him about and they took a hazel branch and teased him, and when he growled they would start laughing. The bear took it all good naturedly, only when they were a bit too rough he would call out:

"Children, leave me alive!
Snow White, Rose Red,
Will you beat your suitor dead?"

When it was bedtime, the mother said to the bear: "You can stay here by the hearth, and you will be safe from the cold and the bad weather." As soon as daylight came the two children let the bear out, and he trotted across the snow into the forest.

And so, all winter the bear came every evening at exactly the same time. He would lie down by the hearth and let the children tease him as much as they liked. They got so used to his coming that the door was never locked until their big brown bear friend had arrived.

When spring came and all the growing things outside were turning green, the bear said one morning to Snow White: "I must go away now, and cannot come back for the whole summer." "Where are you going, then, dear bear?" asked Snow White. "I must go into the forest and guard my treasures from the wicked dwarfs. In the winter, when the earth is frozen hard, they are forced to stay underground and cannot work their way through it. But now that the sun has warmed the earth, they can break through and come out to pry and steal. Whatever they once get their hands on and carry off to their caves does not easily see the light of day again."

Snow White felt quite sad that he was leaving. As she unbolted the door for him, and the bear was hurrying out, he caught against the bolt, and a piece of his brown fur coat was torn off. It seemed to Snow White as if she had seen gold shimmering through it, but she was not sure about it. The bear hurried off, and was soon out of sight behind the trees.

hortly afterwards, the mother sent the children into the forest to gather firewood. There they came upon a big tree which had fallen to the ground. Near the trunk something was jumping up and down in the grass, but they could not figure out what it was.

When they got closer they saw it was a dwarf with an old withered face and a very long beard that was as white as snow. The end of his beard was caught in a crack of the tree trunk, and the little fellow was jumping about like a dog tied to a rope, and didn't know what to do.

He glared at the two girls with his fiery red eyes and cried out: "Why are you just standing there? Can you not come here and help me?" "What happened to you, little man?" asked Rose Red. "Oh, you stupid, prying goose!" retorted the dwarf. "If you must know, I wanted to split the tree trunk to get some small pieces of wood for cooking. The little bit of food that we dwarves eat would burn up immediately in the heat of big logs. We don't need so much to eat as you coarse, greedy folk. I had just driven the wedge in exactly the right spot, and everything was going well, but the stupid wedge was too smooth and suddenly popped out. The crack closed so quickly that I couldn't pull out my beautiful white beard, and now it is tightly held and I can't get away. And you silly, milk-faced things just stand there and laugh! Ugh! How odious you both are!"

The children tried very hard, but they couldn't pull the beard out. "I'll run and get help," said Rose Red. "You senseless goose!" snarled the dwarf. "Why should you get someone else? You are already two too many for me. Can't you think of something better?" "Don't be impatient," said Snow White, "I will help you." And she pulled a little pair of scissors out of her pocket and cut off the end of the beard.

As soon as the dwarf realized he was free, he grabbed a bag, which was filled with gold, that was hanging on a branch of the fallen tree. He lifted it up, grumbling to himself, "Uncouth brats, to cut off a piece of my fine beard. Bad luck to you!" Then he swung the bag onto his back and went off without even once looking at the children.

oon afterwards Snow White and Rose Red went to catch some fish for dinner. As they got near the brook they saw something that looked like a large grasshopper hopping toward the water, as if it were going to jump in. They ran to get a closer look and found it was the dwarf. "Where are you going?" said Rose Red. "You surely don't want to go into the water, do you?" "I am not such a fool!" cried the dwarf. "Don't you see that I am being pulled by the accursed fish?"

The dwarf had been sitting there fishing, and unluckily the wind had tangled up his beard with the fishing line just as the big fish made a bite. The scrawny little dwarf didn't have the strength to pull the fish out of the water and now, although the dwarf held onto the reeds and rushes with all his might, it was of little good, and he was in urgent danger of being dragged into the water.

The girls had come just in time. They held onto him and tried to free his beard from the line, but it was no use. There was nothing to do but to take out the little pair of scissors again and cut the beard, leaving a little bit of it on the fishing line. When the dwarf saw that, he screamed at them: "Is that civil, you nasty little toads, to disfigure my face? Was it not enough to clip off the end of my beard? Now you have cut off the best part of it. I cannot let myself be seen at home. I wish you were forced to run the soles off your shoes!" With that, he grabbed a sack of pearls that he had hidden in the rushes, and without another word he dragged it away and disappeared beneath a rock.

One day, not long afterwards, the mother sent the two children into the town to buy needles and thread and laces and ribbons. The road led them across a heath that had huge rocks strewn all over it. Suddenly they noticed an eagle hovering in the air above them, flying slowly round and round. It sank lower and lower, and at last settled on a rock not far away. A moment later, they heard a loud, pitiful cry. They ran up and saw with horror that the eagle had seized their old acquaintance, the dwarf, and was going to carry him off.

The kindhearted children at once took a tight hold of the little man, and struggled against the eagle until at last he let go of his prize. As soon as the dwarf had recovered from his fright, he cried with his shrill voice: "Could you not have done it more carefully? Look at my coat! You pulled at it so hard that now it's all torn and full of holes, you clumsy creatures!"

Then he took up a sack full of precious jewels and slipped away again under the rock into his hole. By this time, the girls were used to his ingratitude, and they simply continued on their way to town.

s they crossed the heath again on their way home, they surprised the dwarf, who had just emptied out his bag of precious jewels to count them in a sheltered spot. He had not thought that anyone would be passing by so late. The evening sun was shining on the precious stones, so that they glittered and sparkled brilliantly. The children stood still and stared at them. "Why do you stand gaping there?" cried the dwarf, and his ashen-grey face turned copper-red with rage. He was still cursing loudly when a low growling filled the air, and out of the forest rushed a huge brown bear. The dwarf jumped up in a fright, but he could not reach his cave in time, for the bear was quick. Terrified, he cried out: "Dear Mr. Bear, spare me and I will give you all my treasures. Look at all the beautiful jewels lying there! Give me my life! What do you want with such a little fellow like me? You would not even feel me between your teeth. Take these two wicked girls instead. They are tender morsels for you, fat as young quails. For mercy's sake, eat them!" The bear paid no attention to his words, but gave the wicked creature a single blow with his paw, and after that the dwarf didn't move again.

The girls had run away, but the bear called out to them: "Snow White and Rose Red, don't be afraid. Wait for me, and I will come with you." They recognized his voice and stood still.

When he caught up to them, his bearskin fell off, and he stood there, suddenly, as a handsome youth, clothed all in gold. "I am a king's son," he said, "and that wicked dwarf stole my treasure and turned me into a wild bear. I was forced to roam the forest until his death broke the spell. Now he has gotten the punishment he deserved.

After a few years, Snow White married the prince and Rose Red married his brother, and they shared between them the great treasure that the dwarf had gathered together in his cave. The old mother lived with her children

for many years in peace and happiness. She brought with her from the cottage the two rose-trees and planted them in front of her window, where every year they bore the most beautiful roses, white and red.

The

End

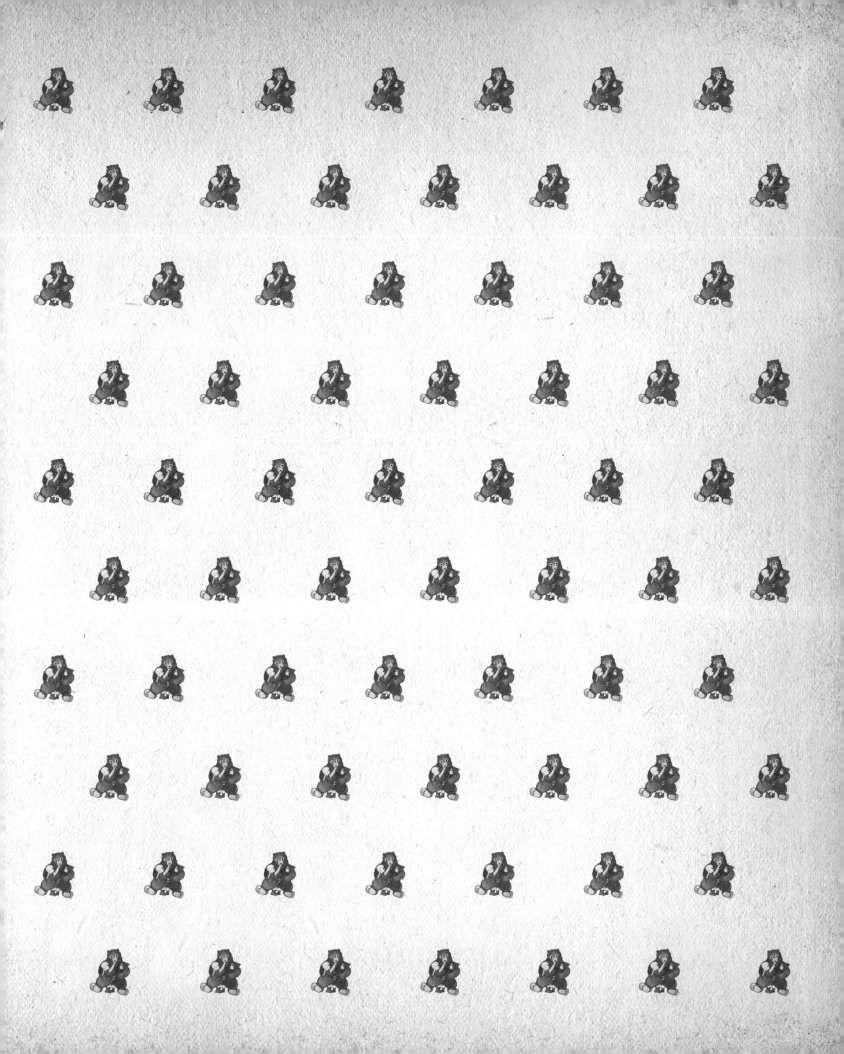

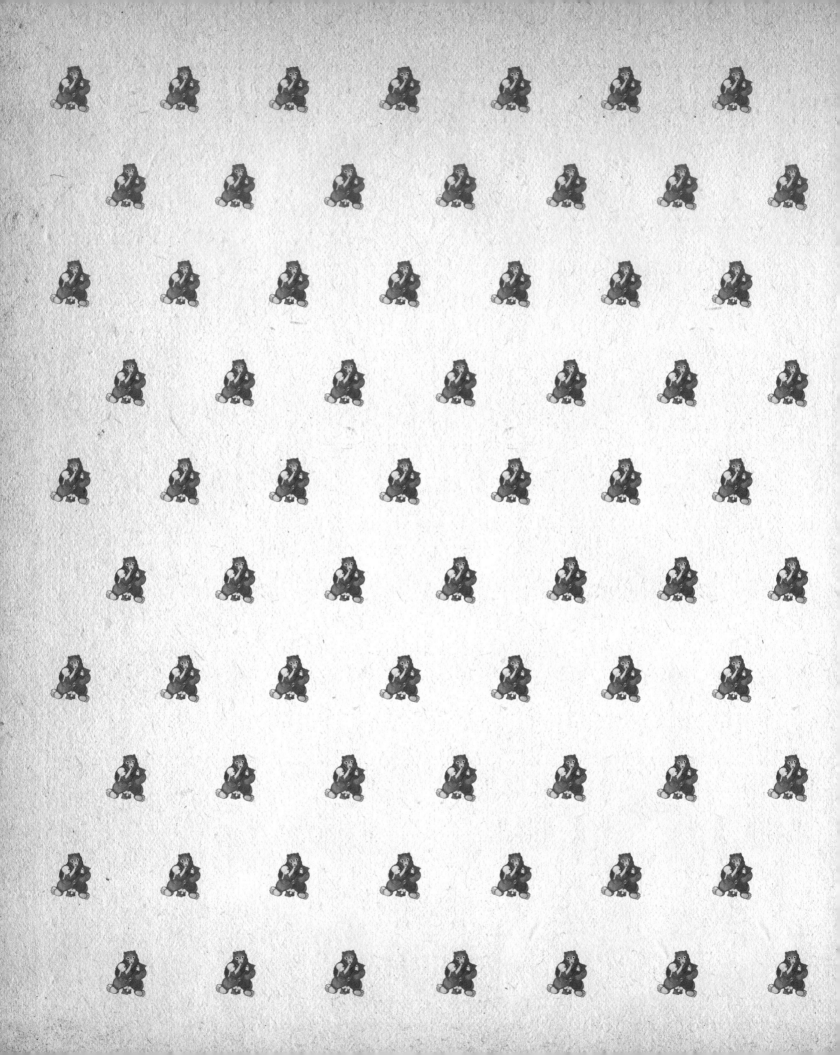